Rapunzel

Miles Kelly

Once there was a man and a woman who lived in a lovely cottage. It was perfect, except for one thing...

...their neighbour was a powerful witch.

One day the couple found out that they were going to have a baby. They set to work to get the nursery ready.

The room had a view of the witch's splendid garden.

The man was worried that his wife would die if she did not taste the lettuce – it seemed to have **bewitched** her.

At twilight, he clambered over the high wall into the witch's garden and grabbed a handful of lettuce.

That night they made a salad, and his wife ate it all. It tasted so good that the next day she longed for it three times as much as before.

So the man returned to the witch's garden. But as soon as he grabbed the lettuce a voice rang out,

"How dare you steal from me!"

The man stuttered that he had been afraid his wife would die if she could not eat the lettuce.

The witch thought this over. "If your wife will die without it, you may take as much of it as you like.

"In return you must give me your child when it is born. I shall be a mother to it."

In his panic the man agreed. He returned to his wife and sadly told her of his promise.

The couple were heartbroken, but they could think of no way out of the bargain.

A few months later their baby – a little girl – was born. The witch appeared at once, and took the child away with her.

The witch named the baby Rapunzel. They lived in a magic tower deep in a forest. It had no stairs or door – only a single window at the very top.

Rapunzel grew into a lovely girl, with long, thick hair. As the years passed, it grew longer... and longer... and longer.

It grew so long that instead of using magic to get into the tower, the witch could just call,

"Rapunzel, Rapunzel, let down your hair."

Rapunzel would hang her braid out of the window and the witch would climb up it.

One day a prince was riding through the forest when he heard beautiful singing. He followed it, and found the tower.

When he saw the witch, the prince hid. He heard her call, saw the braid tumble down and watched her climb up.

The prince waited for the witch to leave, and then did his best to copy the call.

"Rapunzel, Rapunzel, let down your hair."

To his delight, the braid came tumbling out of the window, and up he climbed.

At first Rapunzel was scared, but the prince was so kind that she quickly lost her fears. She told him of her lonely life in the tower.

"I must escape!" she told him.

The prince agreed to come back the next evening with a rope so they could escape together.

But when the witch returned she spotted a flower that the prince had given to Rapunzel. She knew at once that someone had been in the tower.

She cut off Rapunzel's braid and cast a spell that sent Rapunzel to faraway mountains.

When evening came, the witch heard the prince calling from the bottom of the tower.

She let down the braid...

...and as the prince reached the window she cast her spell.

The spell caught the prince in the eyes, blinding him. He let go of the braid and fell, landing in some bushes far below.

Battered and bruised, the prince set off through the forest to find Rapunzel.

Behind him he heard a crumbling, creaking sound. The witch's anger had caused the tower to crack.

It tumbled to the ground –
and that was the end of her.

One day, after many miles of walking,
the prince heard a faint voice singing
on the wind, and he followed it.

He came to a little house set among
the mountains. It was here that the
singing was coming from.

It was Rapunzel's voice the prince could hear!
Her tears of joy at the sight of him fell on the
prince's eyes and he found that he could see again.

The pair set off together
to the prince's castle.

Rapunzel's parents came to the wedding and it was a day of great joy. And they all lived happily together ever after.

Hooray!